Fables

The Fox and the Goat

Retold by Jeffery L. Williams

Illustrated by Alessandro Pastori

HAMERAY PUBLISHING GROUP

Little Goat liked to jump.

She jumped on the fence.
She jumped on the rocks.
She even jumped on her father.

Help!

One day, Little Goat was jumping on a tree stump.
She heard someone yell, "Help!" It was coming
from the well.

4

Little Goat jumped up onto the well and looked
down. She could see Mr. Fox in the water.

"Hello, Mr. Fox!" she yelled. "You must be having fun swimming! Is the water cold?"

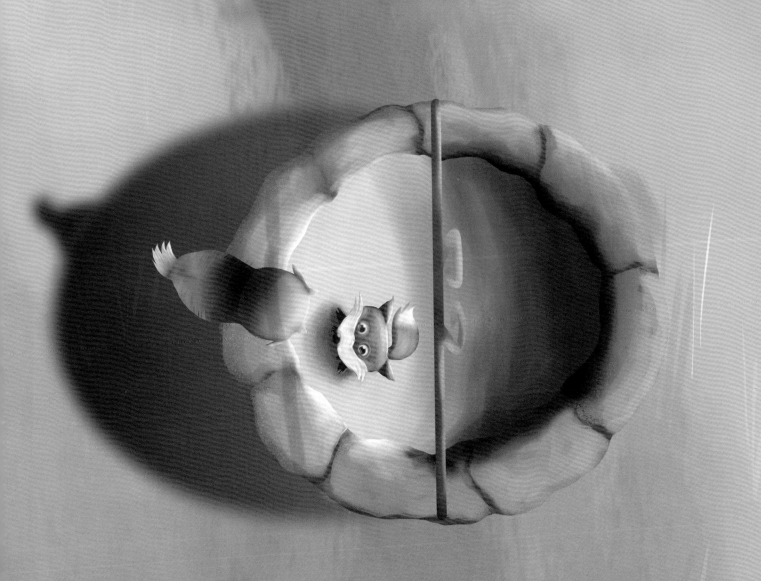

"It is cold," said Mr. Fox, "but I fell in and I need you to help me get . . ."

Splash! Little Goat jumped into the well before she heard what Mr. Fox was saying.

8

Little Goat jumped and jumped and jumped.
She splashed and splashed and splashed.

But Mr. Fox cried and cried and cried.
"What's wrong?" asked Little Goat. "Why are
you crying?"

"I was trying to tell you that I needed help to get out of the well. Now we are both stuck!"

"Oh, no!" said Little Goat. "What will we do?"
she asked, as she jumped onto Mr. Fox.

Then Mr. Fox had an idea. "Little Goat, can you
climb onto my head and jump out of the . . . "

Before he could finish, Little Goat climbed up
on his head and jumped out!

Then she pulled Mr. Fox out of the well in a bucket. "Thank you, Little Goat!" said Mr. Fox. "I hope you learned a lesson."

"Yes, I did!" said Little Goat. "I learned that you need to look and think before you jump into something!"